THE GRUMPY FRUMPY CROISSANT

By Mona K
Illustrations by Korey Scott

Printed in the United States of America

ISBN 978-1-7359308-0-0 (hardcover)
ISBN 978-1-7359308-2-4 (paperback)
ISBN 978-1-7359308-1-7 (ebook)

**Canoe Tree
Press**

4697 Main Street
Manchester Center, VT 05255

Canoe Tree Press is a division of DartFrog Books.

Croissant, Toast, Scone, and Milk are good friends. They all lived together on a kitchen table in the kitchen.

One morning Croissant was feeling grumpy,
because Toast and Scone
were put on the breakfast plate first.

Croissant had to balance on the edge of the plate because there was no room for him on the plate. He felt cross.

8

He didn't talk to Toast and Scone when they brightly said, "Good Morning."

10

He noticed Croissant was so angry that his butter started melting. Croissant was shrinking.

"What's the matter, Croissant?" Milk asked.

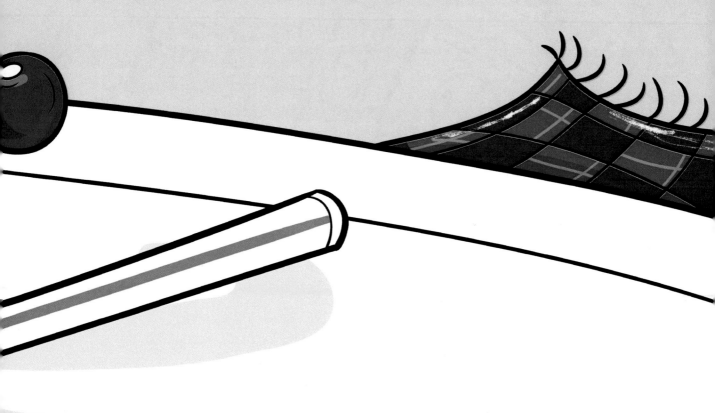

"Toast and Scone are being mean to me," Croissant cried.

"You're being mean because you're taking up all the room on the plate," Croissant argued.

18

"OK, calm down," Milk sighed. "Everyone have a sip of me and take ten deep breaths."

Croissant slurped some milk.
He counted ten deep breaths.
So did Toast and Scone.

6

7

8

9

10

23

"How do you feel Croissant?" Milk asked.
"A bit calmer now? Happier?"

"Yes, thank you," Croissant nodded. He filled himself with butter again. Toast and Scone were happier too. They both moved up on the plate so Croissant had more room to stretch out. He smiled gratefully at them.

Croissant, Toast and Scone lived happily on the plate together and if they ever felt grumpy, all they needed was a drink of milk and a count to ten.

Ingredients

- Makes 10 croissants
- 2 cups strong bread flour
- 1 stick cold unsalted butter, cubed
- 1/2 cup lukewarm milk
- 3 tbsp sugar
- 7 g- active dry yeast
- 1/2 tsp salt
- Egg Wash
- 1 egg yolk
- 1 tbsp milk

1. Pour the flour, salt in a deep bowl.
Mix, Mix, Mix

2. Put the yeast in a bowl with the lukewarm milk
and sugar. Mix, Mix, Mix until the yeast dissolves

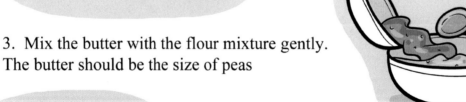

3. Mix the butter with the flour mixture gently.
The butter should be the size of peas

4. Put the yeast liquid mixture to the dry flour mixture
and gently mix until a dough is formed. Don't mix too har
Make a square and put the dough in a plastic wrap.
Refrigerate for one hour

5. Dust your work surface and rolling pin with flour.
Roll the dough into a rectangle.Fold the shorter sides
into the middle. Fold the top and bottom like a pouch.

6. Flip the dough such that the seams are underneath.
Repeat the rolling and folding 4-5 times.
Wrap the dough and refrigerate overnight

7. On a lightly floured surface, roll a rectangle about
10 inches by 16 inches.
Cut the dough into 10 triangles with a pizza cutter.
Shape into croissants.
Keep on a parchment paper and let the croissants rise
for 3-4 hours

8. Preheat the oven to 450 F.
Egg wash the croissants

9. Bake the croissants for 7 minutes.
Reduce the temperature to 375 F and bake
for 14 minutes until golden brown

10. Cool before enjoying with Jelly
or More Butter

32

Made in the USA
Middletown, DE
01 May 2021